# FOR PIA AND ISABEL

*Library of Congress Cataloging-in-Publication Data*

Potter, Giselle, author, illustrator.

Tell me what to dream about / Giselle Potter. — First edition.

pages cm

Summary: At bedtime, a little girl asks her big sister to tell her what to dream about

and together they imagine the possibilities.

ISBN 978-0-385-37423-1 (hardcover) — ISBN 978-0-385-37424-8 (glb) —

ISBN 978-0-385-37425-5 (ebook)

[1. Imagination—Fiction. 2. Sisters—Fiction. 3. Bedtime—Fiction.

4. Dreams—Fiction.] I. Title.

PZ7.P8519Tel 2015

[E]—dc23

2013018302

The text of this book is set in Strangelove.

The illustrations were rendered in watercolor and ink.

Book design by Rachael Cole

MANUFACTURED IN CHINA

2 4 6 8 10 9 7 5 3 1

First Edition

# TELL ME WHAT TO DREAM ABOUT

## GISELLE POTTER

schwartz & wade books · new york

"Tell me what to dream about
or I won't be able to fall asleep,"
a little girl said to her big sister.

"Just close your eyes," the big sister replied.

"I can't! Please?" begged the little girl.

"Okay, fine. Why don't you dream about having waffles for breakfast?"

"That's not a good dream!" said the little girl.

"Then how about you're having teeny-tiny waffles with teeny-tiny animals?"

"Yuck! I don't want little animals crawling all over my waffles."

The big sister tried again.

"What if the animals aren't tiny but *you're* big? Actually, you are a giant with lots of cute, furry pets that fit in your pockets. When you carry them around, they sing in funny squeaky voices. *Deedley dum dee dee . . .*"

"No way!" said the little girl. "I definitely
don't want to be a giant with squeaky pets."
"Fine," said the big sister. "How about . . .

". . . you live in a furry world. *Everything* is furry.
Your clothes and shoes are all furry. Your house
is furry. Your floors and walls and ceiling are furry.
Your friends are all furry, and they come over to
your furry house to have fur parties."

"Furry friends might be scary, and then
I'll have scary dreams," said the little girl.

"Hmmm," said the big sister. "Okay . . .

". . . instead of a furry world, it is a *fluffy* world. You live in the clouds. You can ride them around the sky and they are so soft, and if you are cold you can wear one like a sweater and it will keep you so warm, and if you get hungry you can eat one and it will melt in your mouth like cotton candy."

The big sister liked her own idea a lot, but . . .

. . . the little girl did not.
"It would be scary to live so high up."

"Ai-yi-yi!" said the big sister. "Well then . . .

"... instead of way up in the clouds, you live in a
tree-house town. Everyone lives in tree houses,
and the grocery store is a tree house. Our school,
our favorite restaurant, and everything is in the trees.
There are swings everywhere, and you can swing from
one tree house to another to visit your friends."

The little girl was worried about this dream. "What if it turns into a nightmare where I'm falling out of my tree house?"

"Ugh!" said the big sister. "Okay, then . . . .

". . . you're tiny and live in a tiny moss house *under* a tree. You collect raspberries and blueberries from the bushes. You are so tiny you only need one of each to fill up your tiny tummy. You make dresses out of leaves and flowers and wear a mushroom cap for a hat."

"Are you tiny and live with me too?" the little girl wondered.

"Yes. I am tiny too, but I'm bigger than you."

"How about we live with lots of babies and puppies also?"

"Sure," said the big sister, "but do you want *me* to tell you what to dream about, or are *you* just going to do it?"

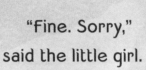

"Fine. Sorry,"
said the little girl.

"Now I forgot what I was saying," said the
big sister. "I'll just have to start over.

"Okay, dream about when we grow up and we live together in a pretty blue house with two puppies, one white with black spots and one black with white spots. Our backyard will be a playground with slides and a tire swing. And our job is to take care of babies. Like a baby school and we're teachers. I'll be the main teacher, and you can be the helper."

"I don't want to be the helper,"
said the little girl.

The big sister yawned. "Well, I'm too tired to think of anything else."

"I have an idea. Let's just dream about making waffles for breakfast, okay?" said the little girl.

"Mmm-hmmmm."

"Are you dreaming about that?"

"Mmm-hmmmm."

"Me too," said the little girl.
But nobody could hear her, because
both sisters were fast asleep.